Edward -or- Jacob

Quick Quizzes for Fans of the Twilight saga

By Riley Brooks

SCHOLASTIC INC.

New York   Toronto   London   Auckland
Sydney   Mexico City   New Delhi   Hong Kong

Photo Credits: Cover, lft: © Paul Fenton/ZUMA Press, rt: © Jordan Strauss/WireImage/Getty Images, ribbon: © Mark Wragg/iStockphoto; Back Cover, lft: © Matt Sayles/AP Photo, rt: © Evan Agostini/AP Photo; Pages 2-3: © NFZ/Reflexstock; Pages 4-11: © Rey Kaminsky/NFZ/Reflexstock; Page 12 top: © Kevin Winter/Getty Images, bot: © Matt Sayles/AP Photo; Page 13: © Dennis Van Tine/Retna Ltd./Corbis; Pages 14-21: © NFZ/Reflexstock; Page 22, bot rt: © Michael Tran/FilmMagic/Getty Images, left: © Dan Steinberg/AP Photo, top rt: © Gregg DeGuire/PictureGroup/AP Images; Page 23: © Jordan Strauss/WireImage/Getty Images; Pages 24-31: © Aldona Martin/NFZ/Reflexstock; Page 32, top: © David Livingston/Getty Images, bot: © DZILLA/BauerGriffin; Page 33: © Jeffrey Mayer/WireImage/Getty Images; Pages 34-41: © Stepan Popov/NFZ/Reflexstock; Page 42: © Hubert Boesl/Newscom; Page 43: © John Barrett/Globe Photos/Zuma Press; Pages 44-51: © Denis Pepin/NFZ/Reflexstock; Page 52: © Vince Gonzales/FilmMagic/Getty Images; Page 53: © WENN/Newscom; Pages 54-61: © NFZ/Reflexstock; Page 62, bot: © Stewart Cook/Rex USA, top: © Sara De Boer/Retna Ltd./Corbis; Page 63: © Jason Merritt/Getty Images; Pages 64-71: © NFZ/Reflexstock; Page 72, bot lft: © Jordan Strauss/Getty Images, middle: © Gary Gershoff/WireImage/Getty Images, top lft: © Carlos Alvarez/Getty Images; Page 73: © Steve Granitz/WireImage/Getty Images; Pages 74-81: © Corel RF; Page 82: © Hutchins Photo/Newscom; Page 83, bot lft: © Bitte Fotovermerk/Rex USA, top: © Jim Smeal/BEImages; Pages 84-91: © Herbert Kratky/NFZ/Reflexstock; Page 92, bot: © Michael Buckner/Getty Images for Summit Entertainment, top: © Imprint Entertainment/Maverick Films/Summit Entertainment/Album/Newscom; Page 93: © Chelsea Lauren/WireImage/Getty Images; Pages 94-95: © Stepan Popov/NFZ/Reflexstock; Page 96, bot rt: © Jeffrey Mayer/WireImage/Getty Image, top lft: © Sipa/AP Images; Red ribbon pp. 1, 12, 22, 32, 52, 62, 72, 92, 96: © Airyelf/istockphoto; Apple pp. 14-15, 16-17, 18-19, 20-21: © ZoneCreative/istockphoto.

ISBN 978-0-545-24842-6

12 11 10 9 8 7 6 5 4 3 2 1   10 11 12 13 14 15/0

Printed in the U.S.A.
First printing, March 2010
Book designed by Two Red Shoes Design

40

Vampires or werewolves?

The woods or the beach?

Sunshine or shade?

Do you choose friends who are just like you, or friends who have different tastes?

Take these quizzes, and then give them to your friends. How do they compare to you? Circle your answers or fill in the blanks. Quizzes are a fun way to learn about the people you hang out with.

Enjoy!

TWILIGHT TRIVIA

How do you feel about the world of Twilight?

1) *Edward* or *Jacob*?

2) Do you believe in supernatural creatures in general? Y or N

3) Alice or Rosalie?

4) Do you prefer werewolves or vampires or humans?

5) Washington or Arizona?

6) Would you rather live with your mom or dad?

7) Grow old or stay young forever?

8) **Clumsy** or *graceful*?

9) Would you rather have a boyfriend or hang with the girls?

10) Quiet dinner or loud party?

11) Cold skin or warm?

12) Would you rather be well protected or allowed to run wild?

13) **Old-fashioned** or modern?

14) Sun-loving or shade?

15) Drive an old truck or a flashy sports car?

16) Would you rather ride motorcycles or go cliff diving to hear Edward's voice?

17) COLLEGE or **VAMPIRE LIFE**?

Name: Tiana

18) Find true love **now**? Or when you are *older*?

19) Gold eyes or red eyes?

20) The Twilight Saga books or the Twilight Saga movies?

21) America or Italy?

22) Would you believe him if your crush told you he was a vampire? Y or N

23) The **woods** or the beach?

24) New and mysterious, or old and familiar?

25) Would you rather be a vampire or a werewolf?

26) For a first date with a vampire, would you rather go for a quiet Italian dinner or a walk in the woods?

27) For a first date with a werewolf, would you rather go for a walk on the beach or work on a motorcycle?

28) **Fighter** or pacifist?

29) Would you rather **die** to be with a **vampire** or live and love a **werewolf**?

30) If you were Bella, what daredevil stunt would you have done to hear Edward's voice? _____
_____
_____
_____

TWILIGHT TRIVIA

How do you feel about the world of Twilight?

1) *Edward* or Jacob?

2) Do you believe in supernatural creatures in general? Y or N

3) Alice or Rosalie?

4) Do you prefer werewolves or vampires or humans?

5) Washington or Arizona?

6) Would you rather live with your mom or dad?

7) Grow old or stay young forever?

8) **Clumsy** or *graceful*?

9) Would you rather have a boyfriend or hang with the girls?

10) Quiet dinner or loud party?

11) Cold skin or warm?

12) Would you rather be well protected or allowed to run wild?

13) *Old-fashioned* or modern?

14) Sun-loving or shade?

15) Drive an old truck or a flashy sports car?

16) Would you rather ride motorcycles or go cliff diving to hear Edward's voice?

17) COLLEGE or **VAMPIRE LIFE**?

Name:

18) Find true love **now**? Or when you are *older*?

19) Gold eyes or red eyes?

20) The Twilight Saga books or the Twilight Saga movies?

21) America or Italy?

22) Would you believe him if your crush told you he was a vampire? Y or N

23) The **woods** or the beach?

24) New and mysterious, or old and familiar?

25) Would you rather be a vampire or a werewolf?

26) For a first date with a vampire, would you rather go for a quiet Italian dinner or a walk in the woods?

27) For a first date with a werewolf, would you rather go for a walk on the beach or work on a motorcycle?

28) **Fighter** or pacifist?

29) Would you rather **die** to be with a **vampire** or live and love a **werewolf**?

30) If you were Bella, what daredevil stunt would you have done to hear Edward's voice? _____

_____

_____

_____

_____

TWILIGHT TRIVIA

How do you feel about the world of Twilight?

1) *Edward* or *Jacob*?

2) Do you believe in supernatural creatures in general? Y or N

3) Alice or Rosalie?

4) Do you prefer werewolves or vampires or humans?

5) Washington or Arizona?

6) Would you rather live with your mom or dad?

7) Grow old or stay young forever?

8) **Clumsy** or *graceful*?

9) Would you rather have a boyfriend or hang with the girls?

10) Quiet dinner or loud party?

11) Cold skin or warm?

12) Would you rather be well protected or allowed to run wild?

13) **Old-fashioned** or modern?

14) Sun-loving or shade?

15) Drive an old truck or a flashy sports car?

16) Would you rather ride motorcycles or go cliff diving to hear Edward's voice?

17) COLLEGE or **VAMPIRE LIFE**?

18) Find true love **now**? Or when you are *older*?

19) Gold eyes or red eyes?

20) The Twilight Saga books or the Twilight Saga movies?

21) America or Italy?

22) Would you believe him if your crush told you he was a vampire? Y or N

23) The **woods** or the beach?

24) New and mysterious, or old and familiar?

25) Would you rather be a vampire or a werewolf?

26) For a first date with a vampire, would you rather go for a quiet Italian dinner or a walk in the woods?

27) For a first date with a werewolf, would you rather go for a walk on the beach or work on a motorcycle?

28) **Fighter** or pacifist?

29) Would you rather **die** to be with a **vampire** or live and love a **werewolf**?

30) If you were Bella, what daredevil stunt would you have done to hear Edward's voice? _____
_____
_____
_____
_____

TWILIGHT TRIVIA

How do you feel about the world of Twilight?

1) *Edward* or Jacob?

2) Do you believe in supernatural creatures in general? Y or N

3) Alice or Rosalie?

4) Do you prefer werewolves or vampires or humans?

5) Washington or Arizona?

6) Would you rather live with your mom or dad?

7) Grow old or stay young forever?

8) Clumsy or *graceful*?

9) Would you rather have a boyfriend or hang with the girls?

10) Quiet dinner or loud party?

11) Cold skin or warm?

12) Would you rather be well protected or allowed to run wild?

13) Old-fashioned or modern?

14) Sun-loving or shade?

15) Drive an old truck or a flashy sports car?

16) Would you rather ride motorcycles or go cliff diving to hear Edward's voice?

17) COLLEGE or VAMPIRE LIFE?

Name:

18) Find true love **now**? Or when you are *older*?

19) Gold eyes or red eyes?

20) The Twilight Saga books or the Twilight Saga movies?

21) America or Italy?

22) Would you believe him if your crush told you he was a vampire? Y or N

23) The **woods** or the beach?

24) New and mysterious, or old and familiar?

25) Would you rather be a vampire or a werewolf?

26) For a first date with a vampire, would you rather go for a quiet Italian dinner or a walk in the woods?

27) For a first date with a werewolf, would you rather go for a walk on the beach or work on a motorcycle?

28) **Fighter** or pacifist?

29) Would you rather **die** to be with a **vampire** or live and love a **werewolf**?

30) If you were Bella, what daredevil stunt would you have done to hear Edward's voice? _____

_____

_____

_____

VAMPIRE LORE

Are you a fanged fanatic?

1) Who's your fave — Edward or Emmett?

2) Would you rather date a **Vampire** or a human?

3) What's your favorite scent? _____

4) Who's your fave — Emmett or Jasper?

5) Do you think vampires ever have to cut their hair? Y or N

6) Who's your fave —- Jasper or Edward?

7) Which Cullen would you date if you could? _____

8) Who's your fave — Rosalie or Alice?

9) Do you have a *need for speed* or do you like to take it slow?

10) Who's your fave —- Dr. Carlisle or Esme?

11) Would you rather hang out with Rosalie for a day or go to work with Carlisle for a day?

12) Baseball or football?

13) Do you prefer daylight or nighttime?

14) Is your family as **COOL** as the Cullen family? Y or N

15) Which Cullen would you choose to add to your family if you could? _____

16) Do you prefer Stephenie Meyer's vamps or more traditional vampires?

Name: Tiana

17) Do you believe in vampires? Y or N

18) Would you ever dress up as a vampire for Halloween or a costume party? Y or N

19) Would you make the choice to become a vampire if it was offered to you? Y or N

20) How would you feel if you discovered a family member was a vampire? _____

21) Would you crush on a guy you knew was a vampire? Y or N

22) Do you think anyone at school might be a vampire? Y or N

23) Do you think any of your teachers might be a vampire? Y or N

24) Do you think your baseball team would win more games if the players were vampires? Y or N

25) Would you ever vote for a vampire for class president? Y or N

26) Do you think vampires would make straight A's since they can study while everyone else sleeps? Y or N

27) Do you think VAMPIRES like to lie out at the beach? Y or N

28) Which would be prettier — a diamond or a vampire in the sunlight? _____

29) Could you beat a vampire in a staring contest? Y or N

30) What age would you want to be if you ever became a vampire? _____

VAMPIRE LORE

Are you a fanged fanatic?

1) Who's your fave — Edward or Emmett?

2) Would you rather date a **Vampire** or a human?

3) What's your favorite scent? _____

4) Who's your fave — Emmett or Jasper?

5) Do you think vampires ever have to cut their hair? Y or N

6) Who's your fave — Jasper or Edward?

7) Which Cullen would you date if you could? _____

8) Who's your fave — Rosalie or Alice?

9) Do you have a *need for speed* or do you like to take it slow?

10) Who's your fave — Dr. Carlisle or Esme?

11) Would you rather hang out with Rosalie for a day or go to work with Carlisle for a day?

12) Baseball or football?

13) Do you prefer daylight or nighttime?

14) Is your family as **COOL** as the Cullen family? Y or N

15) Which Cullen would you choose to add to your family if you could? _____

16) Do you prefer Stephenie Meyer's vamps or more traditional vampires?

17) Do you believe in vampires? Y or N

18) Would you ever dress up as a vampire for Halloween or a costume party? Y or N

19) Would you make the choice to become a vampire if it was offered to you? Y or N

20) How would you feel if you discovered a family member was a vampire? _____

21) Would you crush on a guy you knew was a vampire? Y or N

22) Do you think anyone at school might be a vampire? Y or N

23) Do you think any of your teachers might be a vampire? Y or N

24) Do you think your baseball team would win more games if the players were vampires? Y or N

25) Would you ever vote for a vampire for class president? Y or N

26) Do you think vampires would make straight A's since they can study while everyone else sleeps? Y or N

27) Do you think VAMPIRES like to lie out at the beach? Y or N

28) Which would be prettier — a diamond or a vampire in the sunlight? _____

29) Could you beat a vampire in a staring contest? Y or N

30) What age would you want to be if you ever became a vampire? _____

VAMPIRE LORE

Are you a fanged fanatic?

1) Who's your fave — Edward or Emmett?

2) Would you rather date a **Vampire** or a human?

3) What's your favorite scent? _____

4) Who's your fave — Emmett or Jasper?

5) Do you think vampires ever have to cut their hair? Y or N

6) Who's your fave — Jasper or Edward?

7) Which Cullen would you date if you could? _____

8) Who's your fave — Rosalie or Alice?

9) Do you have a *need for speed* or do you like to take it slow?

10) Who's your fave — Dr. Carlisle or Esme?

11) Would you rather hang out with Rosalie for a day or go to work with Carlisle for a day?

12) Baseball or football?

13) Do you prefer daylight or nighttime?

14) Is your family as **COOL** as the Cullen family? Y or N

15) Which Cullen would you choose to add to your family if you could? _____

16) Do you prefer Stephenie Meyer's vamps or more traditional vampires?

Name: _____

17) Do you believe in vampires? Y or N

18) Would you ever dress up as a vampire for Halloween or a costume party? Y or N

19) Would you make the choice to become a vampire if it was offered to you? Y or N

20) How would you feel if you discovered a family member was a vampire? _____

21) Would you crush on a guy you knew was a vampire? Y or N

22) Do you think anyone at school might be a vampire? Y or N

23) Do you think any of your teachers might be a vampire? Y or N

24) Do you think your baseball team would win more games if the players were vampires? Y or N

25) Would you ever vote for a vampire for class president? Y or N

26) Do you think vampires would make straight A's since they can study while everyone else sleeps? Y or N

27) Do you think VAMPIRES like to lie out at the beach? Y or N

28) Which would be prettier — a diamond or a vampire in the sunlight?

29) Could you beat a vampire in a staring contest? Y or N

30) What age would you want to be if you ever became a vampire? _____

VAMPIRE LORE

Are you a fanged fanatic?

1) Who's your fave — Edward or Emmett?

2) Would you rather date a **Vampire** or a human?

3) What's your favorite scent? _____

4) Who's your fave — Emmett or Jasper?

5) Do you think vampires ever have to cut their hair? Y or N

6) Who's your fave — Jasper or Edward?

7) Which Cullen would you date if you could? _____

8) Who's your fave — Rosalie or Alice?

9) Do you have a *need for speed* or do you like to **take it slow?**

10) Who's your fave — Dr. Carlisle or Esme?

11) Would you rather hang out with Rosalie for a day or go to work with Carlisle for a day?

12) Baseball or football?

13) Do you prefer daylight or nighttime?

14) Is your family as **COOL** as the Cullen family? Y or N

15) Which Cullen would you choose to add to your family if you could? _____

16) Do you prefer Stephenie Meyer's vamps or more traditional vampires?

17) Do you believe in vampires? Y or N

18) Would you ever dress up as a vampire for Halloween or a costume party? Y or N

19) Would you make the choice to become a vampire if it was offered to you? Y or N

20) How would you feel if you discovered a family member was a vampire? _____

21) Would you crush on a guy you knew was a vampire? Y or N

22) Do you think anyone at school might be a vampire? Y or N

23) Do you think any of your teachers might be a vampire? Y or N

24) Do you think your baseball team would win more games if the players were vampires? Y or N

25) Would you ever vote for a vampire for class president? Y or N

26) Do you think vampires would make straight A's since they can study while everyone else sleeps? Y or N

27) Do you think VAMPIRES like to lie out at the beach? Y or N

28) Which would be prettier — a diamond or a vampire in the sunlight?

29) Could you beat a vampire in a staring contest? Y or N

30) What age would you want to be if you ever became a vampire? _____

WEREWOLF WISDOM

Do you howl with the wolves?

1) Sam or Jacob?

2) Would you rather date a werewolf or a human?

3) **Motorcycle** or TRUCK?

4) Could you work with an enemy to protect someone you love? Y or N

5) Do you believe in werewolves? Y or N

6) Do you jump into a fight quickly or take your time before committing to a side?

7) Are you RECKLESS or cautious?

8) Would you rather be a shape-shifter like the Quileute wolves or a real "Child of the Moon"?

9) Do you think it would be cool to imprint on someone? Y or N

10) If you could imprint on anyone at school who would it be?
_____   __ _____

11) If you could imprint on any of the characters from the Twilight books who would it be? _____

12) If you could imprint on any of the Twilight actors who would it be? _____

13) Would you be freaked out if you saw someone phase, or would you think it was cool?

14) Would you ever dress up as a WEREWOLF for a costume party? Y or N

15) Would you make the choice to become a werewolf if it was offered to you? Y or N

Name: Tiana

16) Are you a team player? Y or N

17) If you knew there were real werewolves, would you carry silver bullets to protect yourself? Y or N

18) If you were *Leah*, would you stay with the pack? Y or N

19) Who in your school would you most think would be a werewolf? _____

20) Which of your teachers do you think could be a werewolf? _____

21) Would you crush on a guy if you knew he was a werewolf? Y or N

22) Do you think a werewolf could have *curly hair*? Y or N

23) Do you think your football team would win more games if all the players were werewolves? Y or N

24) Would you vote for a werewolf for class president? Y or N

25) If you were dating a werewolf, would you be freaked out to hang out with him in wolf form? Y or N

26) Do you think wolves are cute and cuddly, or scary and ferocious?

27) How would you feel if you found out a family member was a werewolf? _____

28) Do you think werewolves go to the doctor or the vet when they are sick? _____

29) Do you think werewolves have pets? Y or N

30) Do you think werewolves go to the hair stylist or a dog groomer to get fixed up?

WEREWOLF WISDOM

Do you howl with the wolves?

1) Sam or Jacob?

2) Would you rather date a werewolf or a human?

3) **Motorcycle** or TRUCK?

4) Could you work with an enemy to protect someone you love? Y or N

5) Do you believe in werewolves? Y or N

6) Do you jump into a fight quickly or take your time before committing to a side?

7) Are you RECKLESS or cautious?

8) Would you rather be a shape-shifter like the Quileute wolves or a real "Child of the Moon"?

9) Do you think it would be cool to imprint on someone? Y or N

10) If you could imprint on anyone at school who would it be?
_____

11) If you could imprint on any of the characters from the Twilight books who would it be? _____

12) If you could imprint on any of the Twilight actors who would it be? _____

13) Would you be freaked out if you saw someone phase, or would you think it was cool?

14) Would you ever dress up as a WEREWOLF for a costume party? Y or N

15) Would you make the choice to become a werewolf if it was offered to you? Y or N

16) Are you a team player? Y or N

17) If you knew there were real werewolves, would you carry silver bullets to protect yourself? Y or N

18) If you were *Leah*, would you stay with the pack? Y or N

19) Who in your school would you most think would be a werewolf? _____

20) Which of your teachers do you think could be a werewolf?

_____

21) Would you crush on a guy if you knew he was a werewolf? Y or N

22) Do you think a werewolf could have *curly hair*? Y or N

23) Do you think your football team would win more games if all the players were werewolves? Y or N

24) Would you vote for a werewolf for class president? Y or N

25) If you were dating a werewolf, would you be freaked out to hang out with him in wolf form? Y or N

26) Do you think wolves are cute and cuddly, or scary and ferocious?

27) How would you feel if you found out a family member was a werewolf? _____

28) Do you think werewolves go to the doctor or the vet when they are sick? _____

29) Do you think werewolves have pets? Y or N

30) Do you think werewolves go to the hair stylist or a dog groomer to get fixed up?

WEREWOLF WISDOM

Do you howl with the wolves?

1) Sam or Jacob?

2) Would you rather date a werewolf or a human?

3) **Motorcycle** or TRUCK?

4) Could you work with an enemy to protect someone you love? Y or N

5) Do you believe in werewolves? Y or N

6) Do you jump into a fight quickly or take your time before committing to a side?

7) Are you RECKLESS or cautious?

8) Would you rather be a shape-shifter like the Quileute wolves or a real "Child of the Moon"?

9) Do you think it would be cool to imprint on someone? Y or N

10) If you could imprint on anyone at school who would it be?
_____

11) If you could imprint on any of the characters from the Twilight books who would it be? _____

12) If you could imprint on any of the Twilight actors who would it be? _____

13) Would you be freaked out if you saw someone phase, or would you think it was cool?

14) Would you ever dress up as a WEREWOLF for a costume party? Y or N

15) Would you make the choice to become a werewolf if it was offered to you? Y or N

16) Are you a team player? Y or N

17) If you knew there were real werewolves, would you carry silver bullets to protect yourself? Y or N

18) If you were *Leah*, would you stay with the pack? Y or N

19) Who in your school would you most think would be a werewolf? _____

20) Which of your teachers do you think could be a werewolf?

_____

21) Would you crush on a guy if you knew he was a werewolf? Y or N

22) Do you think a werewolf could have *curly hair*? Y or N

23) Do you think your football team would win more games if all the players were werewolves? Y or N

24) Would you vote for a werewolf for class president? Y or N

25) If you were dating a werewolf, would you be freaked out to hang out with him in wolf form? Y or N

26) Do you think wolves are *cute and cuddly*, or *scary and ferocious*?

27) How would you feel if you found out a family member was a werewolf? _____

28) Do you think werewolves go to the doctor or the vet when they are sick? _____

29) Do you think werewolves have pets? Y or N

30) Do you think werewolves go to the hair stylist or a dog groomer to get fixed up?

WEREWOLF WISDOM

Do you howl with the wolves?

1) Sam or Jacob?

2) Would you rather date a werewolf or a human?

3) **Motorcycle** or TRUCK?

4) Could you work with an enemy to protect someone you love? Y or N

5) Do you believe in werewolves? Y or N

6) Do you jump into a fight quickly or take your time before committing to a side?

7) Are you RECKLESS or cautious?

8) Would you rather be a shape-shifter like the Quileute wolves or a real "Child of the Moon"?

9) Do you think it would be cool to imprint on someone? Y or N

10) If you could imprint on anyone at school who would it be?

_____

11) If you could imprint on any of the characters from the Twilight books who would it be? _____

12) If you could imprint on any of the Twilight actors who would it be? _____

13) Would you be freaked out if you saw someone phase, or would you think it was cool?

14) Would you ever dress up as a WEREWOLF for a costume party? Y or N

15) Would you make the choice to become a werewolf if it was offered to you? Y or N

Name:

16) Are you a team player? Y or N

17) If you knew there were real werewolves, would you carry silver bullets to protect yourself? Y or N

18) If you were *Leah*, would you stay with the pack? Y or N

19) Who in your school would you most think would be a werewolf? _____

20) Which of your teachers do you think could be a werewolf?
_____

21) Would you crush on a guy if you knew he was a werewolf? Y or N

22) Do you think a werewolf could have *curly hair*? Y or N

23) Do you think your football team would win more games if all the players were werewolves? Y or N

24) Would you vote for a werewolf for class president? Y or N

25) If you were dating a werewolf, would you be freaked out to hang out with him in wolf form? Y or N

26) Do you think wolves are cute and cuddly, or scary and ferocious?

27) How would you feel if you found out a family member was a werewolf? _____

28) Do you think werewolves go to the doctor or the vet when they are sick? _____

29) Do you think werewolves have pets? Y or N

30) Do you think werewolves go to the hair stylist or a dog groomer to get fixed up?

THROUGH A VAMP'S EYES

If you were a vampire ..

1) Would you rather date another vampire or a human?

2) If you found your one true love, would you turn them into a vampire, too? Y or N

3) What position would you play in vampire baseball? _____
_____

4) What type of car would you buy if you were a Cullen?
_____

5) Would you drink human or animal blood?

6) Would you ever CREATE another vampire? Y or N

7) If you never had to sleep again, what would you do with your spare time? _____

8) What food would you miss eating the most? _____

9) Would you go to high school over and over again if you were a vamp teen? Y or N

10) Would you like to have a special MENTAL POWER? Y or N

11) Which special vamp power is coolest — superspeed or superstrength?

12) Which special vamp power is coolest — skin that sparkles in the sun or a superstrong sense of smell?

13) Which special vamp power is coolest — being able to see clearly for miles or IMMORTALITY?

14) Would you get married over and over again like Rosalie and Emmett, or just once like Jasper and Alice?

Name: _____

15) What would you miss most about being human? _____
_____

16) Would you miss all of your human friends? Y or N

17) Would it bother you to move around so much? Y or N

18) Would you be able to hunt ANiMALS to feed on them? Y or N

19) Would you use your vamp powers to protect humans? Y or N

20) Would you be able to be friendly with werewolves if they knew you didn't drink human blood? Y or N

21) Would you travel around the world or stay in one nice town?

22) Would you travel underwater or over land?

23) Would you prefer to be in a vampire family or on your own?

24) Would you live in a **BIG CITY** or a small town?

25) Would you be able to work in a hospital surrounded by blood like Carlisle? Y or N

26) Would you ever consider joining the Volturi? Y or N

27) Who would you choose to be your vampire teacher as a newborn? _____

28) Would you hate the person who made you a vampire? Y or N

29) Would you spend all your time searching for a soul mate to share eternity with? Y or N

30) Would you miss not being able to have kids one day? Y or N

THROUGH A VAMP'S EYES

If you were a vampire..

1) Would you rather date another vampire or a human?

2) If you found your one true love, would you turn them into a vampire, too? Y or N

3) What position would you play in vampire baseball? _____
   _____

4) What type of car would you buy if you were a Cullen?
   _____

5) Would you drink human or animal blood?

6) Would you ever **CREATE** another vampire? Y or N

7) If you never had to sleep again, what would you do with your spare time? _____

8) What food would you miss eating the most? _____

9) Would you go to high school over and over again if you were a vamp teen? Y or N

10) Would you like to have a special MENTAL POWER? Y or N

11) Which special vamp power is coolest — superspeed or superstrength?

12) Which special vamp power is coolest — skin that sparkles in the sun or a superstrong sense of smell?

13) Which special vamp power is coolest — being able to see clearly for miles or IMMORTALITY?

14) Would you get married over and over again like Rosalie and Emmett, or just once like Jasper and Alice?

Name:

15) What would you miss most about being human? _____
_____

16) Would you miss all of your human friends? Y or N

17) Would it bother you to move around so much? Y or N

18) Would you be able to hunt ANIMALS to feed on them? Y or N

19) Would you use your vamp powers to protect humans? Y or N

20) Would you be able to be friendly with werewolves if they knew you didn't drink human blood? Y or N

21) Would you travel around the world or stay in one nice town?

22) Would you travel underwater or over land?

23) Would you prefer to be in a vampire family or on your own?

24) Would you live in a **BIG CITY** or a small town?

25) Would you be able to work in a hospital surrounded by blood like Carlisle? Y or N

26) Would you ever consider joining the Volturi? Y or N

27) Who would you choose to be your vampire teacher as a newborn? _____

28) Would you hate the person who made you a vampire? Y or N

29) Would you spend all your time searching for a Soul mate to share eternity with? Y or N

30) Would you miss not being able to have kids one day? Y or N

THROUGH A VAMP'S EYES

If you were a vampire...

1) Would you rather date another vampire or a human?

2) If you found your one true love, would you turn them into a vampire, too? Y or N

3) What position would you play in vampire baseball? _____
   _____

4) What type of car would you buy if you were a Cullen?
   _____

5) Would you drink human or animal blood?

6) Would you ever *CREATE* another vampire? Y or N

7) If you never had to sleep again, what would you do with your spare time? _____

8) What food would you miss eating the most? _____

9) Would you go to high school over and over again if you were a vamp teen? Y or N

10) Would you like to have a special MENTAL POWER? Y or N

11) Which special vamp power is coolest — superspeed or superstrength?

12) Which special vamp power is coolest — skin that sparkles in the sun or a superstrong sense of smell?

13) Which special vamp power is coolest — being able to see clearly for miles or IMMORTALITY?

14) Would you get married over and over again like Rosalie and Emmett, or just once like Jasper and Alice?

Name: _____

15) What would you miss most about being human? _____
_____

16) Would you miss all of your human friends? Y or N

17) Would it bother you to move around so much? Y or N

18) Would you be able to hunt ANIMALS to feed on them? Y or N

19) Would you use your vamp powers to protect humans? Y or N

20) Would you be able to be friendly with werewolves if they knew you didn't drink human blood? Y or N

21) Would you travel around the world or stay in one nice town?

22) Would you travel underwater or over land?

23) Would you prefer to be in a vampire family or on your own?

24) Would you live in a **BIG CITY** or a small town?

25) Would you be able to work in a hospital surrounded by blood like Carlisle? Y or N

26) Would you ever consider joining the Volturi? Y or N

27) Who would you choose to be your vampire teacher as a newborn? _____

28) Would you hate the person who made you a vampire? Y or N

29) Would you spend all your time searching for a soul mate to share eternity with? Y or N

30) Would you miss not being able to have kids one day? Y or N

THROUGH A VAMP'S EYES

If you were a vampire . . .

1) Would you rather date another vampire or a human?

2) If you found your one true love, would you turn them into a vampire, too? Y or N

3) What position would you play in vampire baseball? _____ _____

4) What type of car would you buy if you were a Cullen? _____

5) Would you drink human or animal blood?

6) Would you ever CREATE another vampire? Y or N

7) If you never had to sleep again, what would you do with your spare time? _____

8) What food would you miss eating the most? _____

9) Would you go to high school over and over again if you were a vamp teen? Y or N

10) Would you like to have a special MENTAL POWER? Y or N

11) Which special vamp power is coolest — superspeed or superstrength?

12) Which special vamp power is coolest — skin that sparkles in the sun or a superstrong sense of smell?

13) Which special vamp power is coolest — being able to see clearly for miles or IMMORTALITY?

14) Would you get married over and over again like Rosalie and Emmett, or just once like Jasper and Alice?

Name: _____

15) What would you miss most about being human? _____
_____

16) Would you miss all of your human friends? Y or N

17) Would it bother you to move around so much? Y or N

18) Would you be able to hunt ANIMALS to feed on them? Y or N

19) Would you use your vamp powers to protect humans? Y or N

20) Would you be able to be friendly with werewolves if they
knew you didn't drink human blood? Y or N

21) Would you travel around the world or stay in one nice town?

22) Would you travel underwater or over land?

23) Would you prefer to be in a vampire family or on your own?

24) Would you live in a BIG CITY or a small town?

25) Would you be able to work in a hospital surrounded by blood
like Carlisle? Y or N

26) Would you ever consider joining the Volturi? Y or N

27) Who would you choose to be your vampire teacher as
a newborn? _____

28) Would you hate the person who made you a vampire? Y or N

29) Would you spend all your time searching for a soul mate to
share eternity with? Y or N

30) Would you miss not being able to have kids one day? Y or N

THROUGH A WOLF'S EYES

If you were a werewolf . . .

1) Would you be the alpha or just one of the pack?

2) What **COLOR** wolf would you like to be? _____

3) Would you be able to control your thoughts, knowing the rest of the pack could hear you? Y or N

4) Would you stick with the established pack or start your own?

5) Would you rather date another werewolf or a human?

6) Would you prefer wolf form or human form?

7) Would you rather be imprinted or single?

8) Would you change into a wolf and run away to avoid doing chores around the house? Y or N

9) Would you look for someone cool to imprint on? Y or N

10) Would you think it was cool to always know what your pack members were thinking? Y or N

11) Would you rather eat in human form or wolf form?

12) Would you keep your hair short or long?

13) Would you try to find a cure for being a werewolf? Y or N

14) Would you ever howl at the moon? Y or N

15) Would you be able to help protect your pack or would you be afraid to fight?

16) Would you be able to be **FRiENDLY** with vampires if you knew they didn't drink human blood? Y or N

Name: _____

17) Would you have children, knowing they might become werewolves, too? Y or N

18) Would you think being a werewolf was Cool or **SCARY**?

19) Would you use your wolf form to help you learn about nature and other animals? Y or N

20) Would you still be able to hang out with normal humans or would it be weird because they weren't in your pack?

21) Would you rather be in Jacob's pack or Sam's pack?

22) What would be the coolest thing about being a werewolf?
_____

23) Would it be cool to be extra tall and strong in human form?

24) Do you think phasing would be scary the first time it happened? Y or N

25) Would you use your werewolf powers to scare people? Y or N

26) Would you give up your werewolf powers someday to have a normal life? Y or N

27) What embarrassing things would you not want your pack members to hear you thinking? _____

28) What embarrassing things would you not want to hear your pack-mates thinking about? _____

29) Would you want your siblings to be werewolves, too? Y or N

30) Would you tell your friends you were a werewolf or keep it a secret?

THROUGH A WOLF'S EYES

If you were a werewolf . . .

1) Would you be the alpha or just one of the pack?

2) What **COLOr** wolf would you like to be? _____

3) Would you be able to control your thoughts, knowing the rest of the pack could hear you? Y or N

4) Would you stick with the established pack or start your own?

5) Would you rather date another werewolf or a human?

6) Would you prefer wolf form or human form?

7) Would you rather be imprinted or single?

8) Would you change into a wolf and run away to avoid doing chores around the house? Y or N

9) Would you look for SOMEONE COOl to imprint on? Y or N

10) Would you think it was cool to always know what your pack members were thinking? Y or N

11) Would you rather eat in human form or wolf form?

12) Would you keep your hair short or long?

13) Would you try to find a cure for being a werewolf? Y or N

14) Would you ever howl at the moon? Y or N

15) Would you be able to help protect your pack or would you be afraid to fight?

16) Would you be able to be **FRieNDLY** with vampires if you knew they didn't drink human blood? Y or N

Name:

17) Would you have children, knowing they might become werewolves, too? Y or N

18) Would you think being a werewolf was *cool* or **SCARY**?

19) Would you use your wolf form to help you learn about nature and other animals? Y or N

20) Would you still be able to hang out with normal humans or would it be weird because they weren't in your pack?

21) Would you rather be in Jacob's pack or Sam's pack?

22) What would be the coolest thing about being a werewolf?
_____

23) Would it be cool to be extra tall and strong in human form?

24) Do you think **phasing** would be scary the first time it happened? Y or N

25) Would you use your werewolf powers to scare people? Y or N

26) Would you give up your werewolf powers someday to have a normal life? Y or N

27) What embarrassing things would you not want your pack members to hear you thinking? _____

28) What **embarrassing things** would you not want to hear your pack-mates thinking about? _____

29) Would you want your siblings to be werewolves, too? Y or N

30) Would you tell your friends you were a werewolf or keep it a secret?

THROUGH A WOLF'S EYES

If you were a werewolf...

1) Would you be the alpha or just one of the pack?

2) What COLOR wolf would you like to be? _____

3) Would you be able to control your thoughts, knowing the rest of the pack could hear you? Y or N

4) Would you stick with the established pack or start your own?

5) Would you rather date another werewolf or a human?

6) Would you prefer wolf form or human form?

7) Would you rather be imprinted or single?

8) Would you change into a wolf and run away to avoid doing chores around the house? Y or N

9) Would you look for SOMEONE COOL to imprint on? Y or N

10) Would you think it was cool to always know what your pack members were thinking? Y or N

11) Would you rather eat in human form or wolf form?

12) Would you keep your hair short or long?

13) Would you try to find a cure for being a werewolf? Y or N

14) Would you ever howl at the moon? Y or N

15) Would you be able to help protect your pack or would you be afraid to fight?

16) Would you be able to be FRIENDLY with vampires if you knew they didn't drink human blood? Y or N

Name: _____

17) Would you have children, knowing they might become werewolves, too? Y or N

18) Would you think being a werewolf was *Cool* or **SCARY**?

19) Would you use your wolf form to help you learn about nature and other animals? Y or N

20) Would you still be able to hang out with normal humans or would it be weird because they weren't in your pack?

21) Would you rather be in Jacob's pack or Sam's pack?

22) What would be the coolest thing about being a werewolf?

_____

23) Would it be cool to be extra tall and strong in human form?

24) Do you think phasing would be scary the first time it happened? Y or N

25) Would you use your werewolf powers to scare people? Y or N

26) Would you give up your werewolf powers someday to have a normal life? Y or N

27) What embarrassing things would you not want your pack members to hear you thinking? _____

28) What embarrassing things would you not want to hear your pack-mates thinking about? _____

29) Would you want your siblings to be werewolves, too? Y or N

30) Would you tell your friends you were a werewolf or keep it a secret?

THROUGH A WOLF'S EYES

If you were a werewolf...

1) Would you be the alpha or just one of the pack?

2) What **COLOR** wolf would you like to be? _____

3) Would you be able to control your thoughts, knowing the rest of the pack could hear you? Y or N

4) Would you stick with the established pack or start your own?

5) Would you rather date another werewolf or a human?

6) Would you prefer wolf form or human form?

7) Would you rather be imprinted or single?

8) Would you change into a wolf and run away to avoid doing chores around the house? Y or N

9) Would you look for SOMEONE COOL to imprint on? Y or N

10) Would you think it was cool to always know what your pack members were thinking? Y or N

11) Would you rather eat in human form or wolf form?

12) Would you keep your hair short or long?

13) Would you try to find a cure for being a werewolf? Y or N

14) Would you ever howl at the moon? Y or N

15) Would you be able to help protect your pack or would you be afraid to fight?

16) Would you be able to be **FRiENDLY** with vampires if you knew they didn't drink human blood? Y or N

Name:

17) Would you have children, knowing they might become werewolves, too? Y or N

18) Would you think being a werewolf was cool or SCARY?

19) Would you use your wolf form to help you learn about nature and other animals? Y or N

20) Would you still be able to hang out with normal humans or would it be weird because they weren't in your pack?

21) Would you rather be in Jacob's pack or Sam's pack?

22) What would be the coolest thing about being a werewolf?
   _____

23) Would it be cool to be extra tall and strong in human form?

24) Do you think phasing would be scary the first time it happened? Y or N

25) Would you use your werewolf powers to scare people? Y or N

26) Would you give up your werewolf powers someday to have a normal life? Y or N

27) What embarrassing things would you not want your pack members to hear you thinking? _____

28) What embarrassing things would you not want to hear your pack-mates thinking about? _____

29) Would you want your siblings to be werewolves, too? Y or N

30) Would you tell your friends you were a werewolf or keep it a secret?

MIND OVER MATTER

What's your power?

1) Which is cooler — the ability to read minds or the ability to SEE INTO THE FUTURE?

2) Which is cooler — the ability to manipulate other's emotions or the ability to shield people with your mind?

3) Which is cooler — vampire powers or werewolf powers?

4) What special power would you want if you were a vampire?

_____

5) Whose power would you rather have — Alec's or Jane's?

6) Would you rather be supernaturally beautiful like Rosalie or have a special mental power like Edward and Alice?

7) Would it be cool or uncomfortable to read minds? _____

8) If you could read minds, whose mind would you want to read?

_____

9) If you saw the future, would it affect your decisions? Y or N

10) If you could see into the future, do you think you would make fewer mistakes in life? Y or N

11) Would you try to *warn people* if you knew they were about to make a mistake? Y or N

12) Would you try to set two people up if you read their minds and found out that they liked each other? Y or N

13) If you could change people's emotions, would you make your friends happy all the time? Y or N

14) If you could make people see things, would you use your powers to scare them or to make them happy?

15) Would you read your crush's mind to see if he liked you? Y or N

16) What would you do if you read someone's mind and discovered an *embarrassing secret*? _____

17) If you could hurt people with your mind, would you use it to get back at people who were mean to you? Y or N

18) If you could change people's thoughts, would you use your powers to get elected homecoming queen? Y or N

19) If you could change other people's thoughts, would you use your powers to make your crush notice you? Y or N

20) If you knew your best friend could read your mind, would you be able to *stay best friends* with her? Y or N

21) Do you think the ability to read people's minds would cause you to fight with your friends more often? Y or N

22) If you saw the future, would you use it to win the lottery? Y or N

23) If you could see into the future, would you mostly use your powers for personal gain or to help the people you care about?

24) Would you enter the Olympics if you had *SUPERSPEED*? Y or N

25) What mental power not in the books would you like to have?

_____

26) How would that power make your life better? _____

27) How would that power make your life harder? _____

28) How could you use that power to help others? _____

29) Would you rather have a SPECIAL MENTAL POWER or be able to **change shapes**? _____

30) What special traits do you have that you think would become more pronounced when you became a vampire? _____

MIND OVER MATTER

What's your power?

1) Which is cooler — the ability to read minds or the ability to SEE INTO THE FUTURE?

2) Which is cooler — the ability to manipulate other's emotions or the ability to shield people with your mind?

3) Which is cooler — vampire powers or werewolf powers?

4) What special power would you want if you were a vampire?

_____

5) Whose power would you rather have — Alec's or Jane's?

6) Would you rather be supernaturally beautiful like Rosalie or have a special mental power like Edward and Alice?

7) Would it be cool or uncomfortable to read minds? _____

8) If you could read minds, whose mind would you want to read?

_____

9) If you saw the future, would it affect your decisions? Y or N

10) If you could see into the future, do you think you would make fewer mistakes in life? Y or N

11) Would you try to warn people if you knew they were about to make a mistake? Y or N

12) Would you try to set two people up if you read their minds and found out that they liked each other? Y or N

13) If you could change people's emotions, would you make your friends happy all the time? Y or N

14) If you could make people see things, would you use your powers to scare them or to make them happy?

15) Would you read your crush's mind to see if he liked you? Y or N

Name:

16) What would you do if you read someone's mind and discovered an *embarrassing secret*? _____

17) If you could hurt people with your mind, would you use it to get back at people who were mean to you? Y or N

18) If you could change people's thoughts, would you use your powers to get elected homecoming queen? Y or N

19) If you could change other people's thoughts, would you use your powers to make your crush notice you? Y or N

20) If you knew your best friend could read your mind, would you be able to *stay best friends* with her? Y or N

21) Do you think the ability to read people's minds would cause you to fight with your friends more often? Y or N

22) If you saw the future, would you use it to win the lottery? Y or N

23) If you could see into the future, would you mostly use your powers for personal gain or to help the people you care about?

24) Would you enter the Olympics if you had *SUPERSPEED*? Y or N

25) What mental power not in the books would you like to have?

_____

26) How would that power make your life better? _____

27) How would that power make your life harder? _____

28) How could you use that power to help others? _____

29) Would you rather have a SPECIAL MENTAL POWER or be able to **change shapes**? _____

30) What special traits do you have that you think would become more pronounced when you became a vampire? _____

MIND OVER MATTER

What's your power?

1) Which is cooler — the ability to read minds or the ability to SEE INTO THE FUTURE?

2) Which is cooler — the ability to manipulate other's emotions or the ability to shield people with your mind?

3) Which is cooler — vampire powers or werewolf powers?

4) What special power would you want if you were a vampire?

_____

5) Whose power would you rather have — Alec's or Jane's?

6) Would you rather be supernaturally beautiful like Rosalie or have a special mental power like Edward and Alice?

7) Would it be cool or uncomfortable to read minds? _____

8) If you could read minds, whose mind would you want to read?

_____

9) If you saw the future, would it affect your decisions? Y or N

10) If you could see into the future, do you think you would make fewer mistakes in life? Y or N

11) Would you try to *warn people* if you knew they were about to make a mistake? Y or N

12) Would you try to set two people up if you read their minds and found out that they liked each other? Y or N

13) If you could change people's emotions, would you make your friends happy all the time? Y or N

14) If you could make people see things, would you use your powers to scare them or to make them happy?

15) Would you read your crush's mind to see if he liked you? Y or N

Name:

16) What would you do if you read someone's mind and discovered an *embarrassing secret*? _____

17) If you could hurt people with your mind, would you use it to get back at people who were mean to you? Y or N

18) If you could change people's thoughts, would you use your powers to get elected homecoming queen? Y or N

19) If you could change other people's thoughts, would you use your powers to make your crush notice you? Y or N

20) If you knew your best friend could read your mind, would you be able to *stay best friends* with her? Y or N

21) Do you think the ability to read people's minds would cause you to fight with your friends more often? Y or N

22) If you saw the future, would you use it to win the lottery? Y or N

23) If you could see into the future, would you mostly use your powers for personal gain or to help the people you care about?

24) Would you enter the Olympics if you had *SUPERSPEED*? Y or N

25) What mental power not in the books would you like to have?

_____

26) How would that power make your life better? _____

27) How would that power make your life harder? _____

28) How could you use that power to help others? _____

29) Would you rather have a SPECIAL MENTAL POWER or be able to **change shapes**? _____

30) What special traits do you have that you think would become more pronounced when you became a vampire? _____

MiND OVER MATTER

What's your power?

1) Which is cooler — the ability to read minds or the ability to SEE INTO THE FUTURE?

2) Which is cooler — the ability to manipulate other's emotions or the ability to shield people with your mind?

3) Which is cooler — vampire powers or werewolf powers?

4) What special power would you want if you were a vampire?

_____

5) Whose power would you rather have — Alec's or Jane's?

6) Would you rather be supernaturally beautiful like Rosalie or have a special mental power like Edward and Alice?

7) Would it be cool or uncomfortable to read minds? _____

8) If you could read minds, whose mind would you want to read?

_____

9) If you saw the future, would it affect your decisions? Y or N

10) If you could see into the future, do you think you would make fewer mistakes in life? Y or N

11) Would you try to warn people if you knew they were about to make a mistake? Y or N

12) Would you try to set two people up if you read their minds and found out that they liked each other? Y or N

13) If you could change people's emotions, would you make your friends happy all the time? Y or N

14) If you could make people see things, would you use your powers to scare them or to make them happy?

15) Would you read your crush's mind to see if he liked you? Y or N

16) What would you do if you read someone's mind and discovered an *embarrassing secret*? _____

17) If you could hurt people with your mind, would you use it to get back at people who were mean to you? Y or N

18) If you could change people's thoughts, would you use your powers to get elected homecoming queen? Y or N

19) If you could change other people's thoughts, would you use your powers to make your crush notice you? Y or N

20) If you knew your best friend could read your mind, would you be able to *stay best friends* with her? Y or N

21) Do you think the ability to read people's minds would cause you to fight with your friends more often? Y or N

22) If you saw the future, would you use it to win the lottery? Y or N

23) If you could see into the future, would you mostly use your powers for personal gain or to help the people you care about?

24) Would you enter the Olympics if you had *SUPERSPEED*? Y or N

25) What mental power not in the books would you like to have?

_____

26) How would that power make your life better? _____

27) How would that power make your life harder? _____

28) How could you use that power to help others? _____

29) Would you rather have a *SPECIAL MENTAL POWER* or be able to **change shapes**? _____

30) What special traits do you have that you think would become more pronounced when you became a vampire? _____

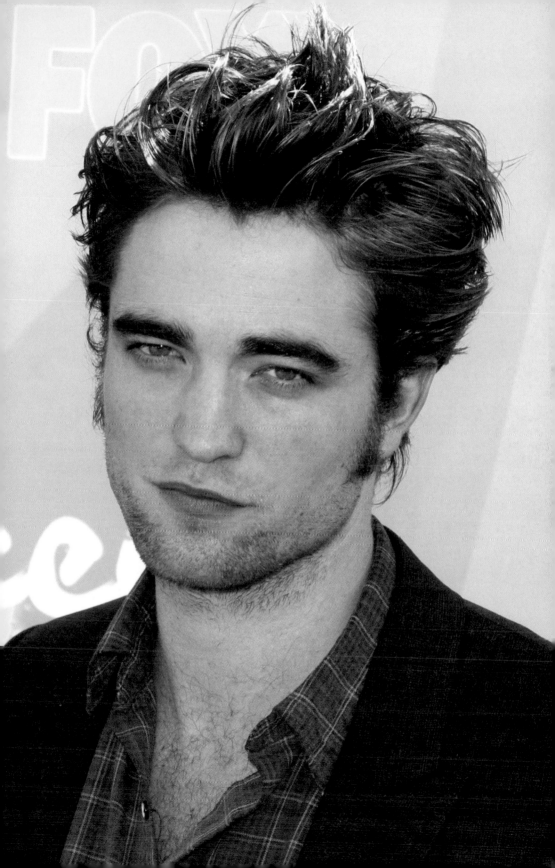

EVERYBODY WAS VAMPIRE FIGHTING

What's your battle style?

1) Which enemy would you rather face — the Volturi or a pack of newborn vamps?

2) In a battle, who would win — the Cullens or the werewolf pack?

3) Is true love worth fighting for? Y or N

4) Do you think the Cullens and the werewolf pack could ever become friends? Y or N

5) Who would you rather fight — James or Victoria?

6) Who would you rather fight — Alec or Jane?

7) Who would you rather arm wrestle — Emmett or Sam?

8) Who would you want to have your back in a fight — Edward or Jacob?

9) Who would you rather fight — James or Laurent?

10) Would you fight a pack of vampires to defend your family? Y or N

11) Would you fight a pack of werewolves to defend your school? Y or N

12) What do you think would be the best weapon to fight vampires with? _A wooden stash_

13) What do you think would be the best weapon to fight werewolves with? _new born vamps_

14) If you encountered a hungry vampire one-on-one, would you try to run and hide or stand and FIGHT?

15) Do you think the Volturi do a good job policing the other vampires? Y or N

Name: 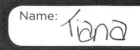 Tiana

16) Which VAMPIRE TRAIT do you think would be the most helpful
in a fight? _mood control + Seeing the future_

17) Which werewolf trait do you think would be the most helpful
in a fight? _strength_

18) If you had to assemble an ultimate fighting team, which five
Twilight characters would you choose? _____
_Emmett, Jasper, Jane_____

19) If Sam and Jacob ever fought, who do you think would win?

20) If Edward and EMMETT ever fought, who do you think
would win?

21) If Leah and Rosalie fought, who do you think would win?

22) Would you help the Cullens if they had to fight the Volturi?
Y or N

23) Do you think all of the american vampires could beat the
Volturi? Y or N

24) Do you think werewolves could beat real wolves in a fight?

25) Do you think the U.S. Army could beat the Volturi in a fight?
No

26) Would you seek out a fight if you were a vampire, or
try to avoid it?

27) Which is scarier — a vampire or a werewolf? ♡LOVE♡

28) What in life is worth fighting for? _____

29) Do you think WAR is necessary? Y or N

30) Could the Cullens have avoided fighting the Volturi by just
explaining about Renesmee? Y or N

What's your battle style?

1) Which enemy would you rather face — the Volturi or a pack of newborn vamps?

2) In a battle, who would win — the Cullens or the werewolf pack?

3) Is true love worth fighting for? Y or N

4) Do you think the Cullens and the werewolf pack could ever become friends? Y or N

5) Who would you rather fight — James or Victoria?

6) Who would you rather fight — Alec or Jane?

7) Who would you rather arm wrestle — Emmett or Sam?

8) Who would you want to have your back in a fight — Edward or Jacob?

9) Who would you rather fight — James or Laurent?

10) Would you fight a pack of vampires to defend your family? Y or N

11) Would you fight a pack of werewolves to **defend your school**? Y or N

12) What do you think would be the best weapon to fight vampires with? _____

13) What do you think would be the best weapon to fight werewolves with? _____

14) If you encountered a hungry vampire one-on-one, would you try to run and hide or stand and FIGHT?

15) Do you think the Volturi do a good job policing the other vampires? Y or N

16) Which VAMPIRE TRAIT do you think would be the most helpful in a fight? _____

17) Which werewolf trait do you think would be the most helpful in a fight? _____

18) If you had to assemble an ultimate fighting team, which five Twilight characters would you choose? _____
_____

19) If Sam and Jacob ever fought, who do you think would win?

20) If Edward and EMMETT ever fought, who do you think would win?

21) If Leah and Rosalie fought, who do you think would win?

22) Would you help the Cullens if they had to fight the Volturi? Y or N

23) Do you think all of the american vampires could beat the Volturi? Y or N

24) Do you think werewolves could beat real wolves in a fight?

25) Do you think the U.S. Army could beat the Volturi in a fight?

26) Would you seek out a fight if you were a vampire, or try to avoid it?

27) Which is scarier — a vampire or a werewolf?

28) What in life is worth fighting for? _____

29) Do you think WAR is necessary? Y or N

30) Could the Cullens have avoided fighting the Volturi by just explaining about Renesmee? Y or N

EVERYBODY WAS VAMPIRE FIGHTING

What's your battle style?

1) Which enemy would you rather face — the Volturi or a pack of newborn vamps?

2) In a battle, who would win — the Cullens or the werewolf pack?

3) Is true love worth fighting for? Y or N

4) Do you think the Cullens and the werewolf pack could ever become friends? Y or N

5) Who would you rather fight — James or Victoria?

6) Who would you rather fight — Alec or Jane?

7) Who would you rather arm wrestle — Emmett or Sam?

8) Who would you want to have your back in a fight — Edward or Jacob?

9) Who would you rather fight — James or Laurent?

10) Would you fight a pack of vampires to defend your family? Y or N

11) Would you fight a pack of werewolves to defend your school? Y or N

12) What do you think would be the best weapon to fight vampires with? _____

13) What do you think would be the best weapon to fight werewolves with? _____

14) If you encountered a hungry vampire one-on-one, would you try to run and hide or stand and FIGHT?

15) Do you think the Volturi do a good job policing the other vampires? Y or N

16) Which VAMPIRE TRAIT do you think would be the most helpful in a fight? _____

17) Which werewolf trait do you think would be the most helpful in a fight? _____

18) If you had to assemble an ultimate fighting team, which five Twilight characters would you choose? _____

_____

19) If Sam and Jacob ever fought, who do you think would win?

20) If Edward and EMMETT ever fought, who do you think would win?

21) If Leah and Rosalie fought, who do you think would win?

22) Would you help the Cullens if they had to fight the Volturi? Y or N

23) Do you think all of the american vampires could beat the Volturi? Y or N

24) Do you think werewolves could beat real wolves in a fight?

25) Do you think the U.S. Army could beat the Volturi in a fight?

26) Would you seek out a fight if you were a vampire, or try to avoid it?

27) Which is scarier — a vampire or a werewolf?

28) What in life is worth fighting for? _____

29) Do you think WAR is necessary? Y or N

30) Could the Cullens have avoided fighting the Volturi by just explaining about Renesmee? Y or N

EVERYBODY WAS VAMPIRE FIGHTING

What's your battle style?

1) Which enemy would you rather face — the Volturi or a pack of newborn vamps?

2) In a battle, who would win — the Cullens or the werewolf pack?

3) Is true love worth fighting for? Y or N

4) Do you think the Cullens and the werewolf pack could ever become friends? Y or N

5) Who would you rather fight — James or Victoria?

6) Who would you rather fight — Alec or Jane?

7) Who would you rather arm wrestle — Emmett or Sam?

8) Who would you want to have your back in a fight — Edward or Jacob?

9) Who would you rather fight — James or Laurent?

10) Would you fight a pack of vampires to defend your family? Y or N

11) Would you fight a pack of werewolves to defend your school? Y or N

12) What do you think would be the best weapon to fight vampires with? _____

13) What do you think would be the best weapon to fight werewolves with? _____

14) If you encountered a hungry vampire one-on-one, would you try to run and hide or stand and FIGHT?

15) Do you think the Volturi do a good job policing the other vampires? Y or N

Name:

16) Which VAMPIRE TRAIT do you think would be the most helpful in a fight? _____

17) Which werewolf trait do you think would be the most helpful in a fight? _____

18) If you had to assemble an ultimate fighting team, which five Twilight characters would you choose? _____
_____

19) If Sam and Jacob ever fought, who do you think would win?

20) If Edward and EMMETT ever fought, who do you think would win?

21) If Leah and Rosalie fought, who do you think would win?

22) Would you help the Cullens if they had to fight the Volturi? Y or N

23) Do you think all of the american vampires could beat the Volturi? Y or N

24) Do you think werewolves could beat real wolves in a fight?

25) Do you think the U.S. Army could beat the Volturi in a fight?

26) Would you seek out a fight if you were a vampire, or try to avoid it?

27) Which is scarier — a vampire or a werewolf?

28) What in life is worth fighting for? _____

29) Do you think WAR is necessary? Y or N

30) Could the Cullens have avoided fighting the Volturi by just explaining about Renesmee? Y or N

TWiLiGHT TRADE-iN

How would you change things?

1) Which Twilight character would you like to be your BFF?

_____

2) Which Twilight character would you like to hang at the mall with? _____

3) Which Twilight character would you like for a prom date?

_____

4) Who would you rather have as a friend if you went to Forks High — Angela or Jessica?

5) Would you rather be Prom Queen or date a Cullen?

6) Would you rather be the most popular girl in school or be a loner who dates the cutest guy in school?

7) Would you rather be friends with Rosalie or Leah?

8) Would you rather play Truth or Dare with Emmett or Jasper?

9) Would you rather study with Alice or Emmett?

10) Would you rather have Renée or Esme for a mom?

11) Would you rather have Charlie or Carlisle for a dad?

12) Would you rather be in the Quileute tribe or just a regular citizen of Forks?

13) Which Twilight character would you let give you a makeover?

_____

14) If you were throwing a party, which five Twilight characters would you invite? _____

_____

15) Which Twilight girl would you vote as Prom Queen? _____

Name:

16) Which Twilight guy would you vote as Prom King? _____

17) Would you **TRADE PLACES WITH BELLA** if you could? Y or N

18) Would you like to visit the real Forks, Washington? Y or N

19) If you were in Bella's situation, what would you do differently?
_____
_____
_____

20) Do you think Bella was strong and smart or a total wimp?

21) Do you think it was selfish of Bella to become a vampire?
Y or N

22) Would you want to have a child who was half-vampire,
half-human? Y or N

23) Do you believe in destiny? Y or N

24) Do you believe in soul mates? Y or N

25) Would you have befriended Bella if she was the new girl at
your school? Y or N

26) Would you date Edward if he asked you out? Y or N

27) Would you date Jacob if he asked you out? Y or N

28) What would you get a vampire for his birthday? _____
_____

29) What would you get a werewolf for his birthday? _____
_____

30) Do you believe in SUPERNATURAL OCCURRENCES? Y or N

TWiLiGHT TRADE-iN

How would you change things?

1) Which Twilight character would you like to be your BFF?
_____

2) Which Twilight character would you like to hang at the mall with? _____

3) Which Twilight character would you like for a prom date?
_____

4) Who would you rather have as a friend if you went to Forks High — Angela or Jessica?

5) Would you rather be Prom Queen or date a Cullen?

6) Would you rather be the most popular girl in school or be a loner who dates the cutest guy in school?

7) Would you rather be friends with Rosalie or Leah?

8) Would you rather play Truth or Dare with Emmett or Jasper?

9) Would you rather study with Alice or Emmett?

10) Would you rather have Renée or Esme for a mom?

11) Would you rather have Charlie or Carlisle for a dad?

12) Would you rather be in the Quileute tribe or just a regular citizen of Forks?

13) Which Twilight character would you let give you a makeover?
_____

14) If you were throwing a party, which five Twilight characters would you invite? _____
_____

15) Which Twilight girl would you vote as Prom Queen? _____

16) Which Twilight guy would you vote as Prom King? _____

17) Would you **TRADE PLACES WITH BELLA** if you could? Y or N

18) Would you like to visit the real Forks, Washington? Y or N

19) If you were in Bella's situation, what would you do differently?
_____
_____
_____

20) Do you think Bella was strong and smart or a total wimp?

21) Do you think it was selfish of Bella to become a vampire? Y or N

22) Would you want to have a child who was half-vampire, half-human? Y or N

23) Do you believe in destiny? Y or N

24) Do you believe in soul mates? Y or N

25) Would you have befriended Bella if she was the new girl at your school? Y or N

26) Would you date Edward if he asked you out? Y or N

27) Would you date Jacob if he asked you out? Y or N

28) What would you get a vampire for his birthday? _____
_____

29) What would you get a werewolf for his birthday? _____
_____

30) Do you believe in SUPERNATURAL OCCURRENCES? Y or N

TWiLiGHT TRADE-iN

How would you change things?

1) Which Twilight character would you like to be your BFF?
_____

2) Which Twilight character would you like to hang at the mall with? _____

3) Which Twilight character would you like for a prom date?
_____

4) Who would you rather have as a friend if you went to Forks High — Angela or Jessica?

5) Would you rather be Prom Queen or date a Cullen?

6) Would you rather be the most popular girl in school or be a loner who dates the cutest guy in school?

7) Would you rather be friends with Rosalie or Leah?

8) Would you rather play Truth or Dare with Emmett or Jasper?

9) Would you rather study with Alice or Emmett?

10) Would you rather have Renée or Esme for a mom?

11) Would you rather have Charlie or Carlisle for a dad?

12) Would you rather be in the Quileute tribe or just a regular citizen of Forks?

13) Which Twilight character would you let give you a makeover?
_____

14) If you were throwing a party, which five Twilight characters would you invite? _____
_____

15) Which Twilight girl would you vote as Prom Queen? _____

Name:

16) Which Twilight guy would you vote as Prom King? _____

17) Would you **TRADE PLACES WITH BELLA** if you could? Y or N

18) Would you like to visit the real Forks, Washington? Y or N

19) If you were in Bella's situation, what would you do differently?
_____
_____
_____

20) Do you think Bella was strong and smart or a total wimp?

21) Do you think it was selfish of Bella to become a vampire?
Y or N

22) Would you want to have a child who was half-vampire,
half-human? Y or N

23) Do you believe in destiny? Y or N

24) Do you believe in soul mates? Y or N

25) Would you have befriended Bella if she was the new girl at
your school? Y or N

26) Would you date Edward if he asked you out? Y or N

27) Would you date Jacob if he asked you out? Y or N

28) What would you get a vampire for his birthday? _____
_____

29) What would you get a werewolf for his birthday? _____
_____

30) Do you believe in SUPERNATURAL OCCURRENCES? Y or N

TWILIGHT TRADE-iN

How would you change things?

1) Which Twilight character would you like to be your BFF?
_____

2) Which Twilight character would you like to hang at the mall with? _____

3) Which Twilight character would you like for a prom date?
_____

4) Who would you rather have as a friend if you went to Forks High — Angela or Jessica?

5) Would you rather be Prom Queen or date a Cullen?

6) Would you rather be the most popular girl in school or be a loner who dates the cutest guy in school?

7) Would you rather be friends with Rosalie or Leah?

8) Would you rather play Truth or Dare with Emmett or Jasper?

9) Would you rather study with Alice or Emmett?

10) Would you rather have Renée or Esme for a mom?

11) Would you rather have Charlie or Carlisle for a dad?

12) Would you rather be in the Quileute tribe or just a regular citizen of Forks?

13) Which Twilight character would you let give you a makeover?
_____

14) If you were throwing a party, which five Twilight characters would you invite? _____
_____

15) Which Twilight girl would you vote as Prom Queen? _____

16) Which Twilight guy would you vote as Prom King? _____

17) Would you **TRADE PLACES WITH BELLA** if you could? Y or N

18) Would you like to visit the real Forks, Washington? Y or N

19) If you were in Bella's situation, what would you do differently?

_____

_____

_____

20) Do you think Bella was strong and smart or a total wimp?

21) Do you think it was selfish of Bella to become a vampire? Y or N

22) Would you want to have a child who was half-vampire, half-human? Y or N

23) Do you believe in destiny? Y or N

24) Do you believe in soul mates? Y or N

25) Would you have befriended Bella if she was the new girl at your school? Y or N

26) Would you date Edward if he asked you out? Y or N

27) Would you date Jacob if he asked you out? Y or N

28) What would you get a vampire for his birthday? _____

_____

29) What would you get a werewolf for his birthday? _____

_____

30) Do you believe in SUPERNATURAL OCCURRENCES? Y or N

MOVIE MOMENTS

How did the movies compare to the books?

1) Was Robert Pattinson the best choice to play Edward Cullen?
Y or N

2) Was kristin stewart the best choice to play Bella Swan?
Y or N

3) Was Kellan Lutz the best choice to play Emmett Cullen?
Y or N

4) Was Nikki Reed the best choice to play Rosalie Hale? Y or N

5) Was Ashley Greene the best choice to play Alice Cullen?
Y or N

6) Was JACKSON RATHBONE the best choice to play Jasper Hale?
Y or N

7) Was Taylor Lautner the best choice to play Jacob Black? Y or N

8) Was Peter Facinelli the best choice to play Carlisle Cullen?
Y or N

9) Was Elizabeth Reaser the best choice to play Esme Cullen?
Y or N

10) If you could be in the movies, which part would you like to play?
_____

11) If you had to cast the movies with your friends, who would you
choose to play each part?_____
_____

12) Which movie is better — Twilight or New Moon?

13) Which movie is better — New Moon or Eclipse?

14) Which movie is better — Eclipse or Twilight?

15) Which actor is cuter — TAYLOR LAUTNER or Robert Pattinson?

16) Which actress is prettier — *Nikki Reed* or ASHLEY GREENE?

17) Which actor is cuter — Jackson Rathbone or Kellan Lutz?

18) Which Twilight actor would you change places with for a day?
_____

19) Which Twilight actor would you like to have visit your school?
_____

20) Which Twilight actor would you like to go to prom with?
_____

21) Which Twilight actor would make the best BFF? _____

22) Which Twilight Saga movie premiere would you have wanted
to attend? _____

23) Which Twilight Saga actor would you like to have for a sibling?
_____

24) What is your fave song from the movie soundtracks? _____
_____

25) What is your fave scene from the movies? _____

26) What is the best quote from the movies? _____

27) If you could change one scene in the movies, which would
it be? _____

28) If you were the director of one of the Twilight movies, what
would you do differently? _____

29) If you could have one Twilight character's wardrobe, whose
would you choose? _____

30) If you could have one Twilight character's car, whose would
you choose? _____

MOVIE MOMENTS

How did the movies compare to the books?

1) Was Robert Pattinson the best choice to play Edward Cullen? Y or N

2) Was kristin stewart the best choice to play Bella Swan? Y or N

3) Was Kellan Lutz the best choice to play Emmett Cullen? Y or N

4) Was Nikki Reed the best choice to play Rosalie Hale? Y or N

5) Was Ashley Greene the best choice to play Alice Cullen? Y or N

6) Was JACKSON RATHBONE the best choice to play Jasper Hale? Y or N

7) Was Taylor Lautner the best choice to play Jacob Black? Y or N

8) Was Peter Facinelli the best choice to play Carlisle Cullen? Y or N

9) Was Elizabeth Reaser the best choice to play Esme Cullen? Y or N

10) If you could be in the movies, which part would you like to play?
_____

11) If you had to cast the movies with your friends, who would you choose to play each part?_____
_____

12) Which movie is better — Twilight or New Moon?

13) Which movie is better — New Moon or Eclipse?

14) Which movie is better — Eclipse or Twilight?

15) Which actor is cuter — TAYLOR LAUTNER or Robert Pattinson?

Name: _____

16) Which actress is prettier — *Nikki Reed* or ASHLEY GREENE?

17) Which actor is cuter — Jackson Rathbone or Kellan Lutz?

18) Which Twilight actor would you change places with for a day?
_____

19) Which Twilight actor would you like to have visit your school?
_____

20) Which Twilight actor would you like to go to prom with?
_____

21) Which Twilight actor would make the best BFF? _____

22) Which Twilight Saga movie premiere would you have wanted to attend? _____

23) Which Twilight Saga actor would you like to have for a sibling?
_____

24) What is your fave song from the movie soundtracks? _____
_____

25) What is your fave scene from the movies? _____

26) What is the best quote from the movies? _____

27) If you could change one scene in the movies, which would it be? _____

28) If you were the director of one of the Twilight movies, what would you do differently? _____

29) If you could have one Twilight character's wardrobe, whose would you choose? _____

30) If you could have one Twilight character's car, whose would you choose? _____

MOVIE MOMENTS

How did the movies compare to the books?

1) Was Robert Pattinson the best choice to play Edward Cullen?
Y or N

2) Was kristin stewart the best choice to play Bella Swan?
Y or N

3) Was Kellan Lutz the best choice to play Emmett Cullen?
Y or N

4) Was Nikki Reed the best choice to play Rosalie Hale? Y or N

5) Was Ashley Greene the best choice to play Alice Cullen?
Y or N

6) Was JACKSON RATHBONE the best choice to play Jasper Hale?
Y or N

7) Was Taylor Lautner the best choice to play Jacob Black? Y or N

8) Was Peter Facinelli the best choice to play Carlisle Cullen?
Y or N

9) Was Elizabeth Reaser the best choice to play Esme Cullen?
Y or N

10) If you could be in the movies, which part would you like to play?

_____

11) If you had to cast the movies with your friends, who would you choose to play each part?_____

_____

12) Which movie is better — *Twilight* or *New Moon*?

13) Which movie is better — *New Moon* or *Eclipse*?

14) Which movie is better — *Eclipse* or *Twilight*?

15) Which actor is cuter — TAYLOR LAUTNER or Robert Pattinson?

Name: _____

16) Which actress is prettier — *Nikki Reed* or ASHLEY GREENE?

17) Which actor is cuter — Jackson Rathbone or Kellan Lutz?

18) Which Twilight actor would you change places with for a day?
_____

19) Which Twilight actor would you like to have visit your school?
_____

20) Which Twilight actor would you like to go to prom with?
_____

21) Which Twilight actor would make the best BFF? _____

22) Which Twilight Saga movie premiere would you have wanted
to attend? _____

23) Which Twilight Saga actor would you like to have for a sibling?
_____

24) What is your fave song from the movie soundtracks? _____
_____

25) What is your fave scene from the movies? _____

26) What is the best quote from the movies? _____

27) If you could change one scene in the movies, which would
it be? _____

28) If you were the director of one of the Twilight movies, what
would you do differently? _____

29) If you could have one Twilight character's wardrobe, whose
would you choose? _____

30) If you could have one Twilight character's car, whose would
you choose? _____

MOVIE MOMENTS

How did the movies compare to the books?

1) Was Robert Pattinson the best choice to play Edward Cullen?
Y or N

2) Was kristin stewart the best choice to play Bella Swan?
Y or N

3) Was Kellan Lutz the best choice to play Emmett Cullen?
Y or N

4) Was Nikki Reed the best choice to play Rosalie Hale? Y or N

5) Was Ashley Greene the best choice to play Alice Cullen?
Y or N

6) Was JACKSON RATHBONE the best choice to play Jasper Hale?
Y or N

7) Was Taylor Lautner the best choice to play Jacob Black? Y or N

8) Was Peter Facinelli the best choice to play Carlisle Cullen?
Y or N

9) Was Elizabeth Reaser the best choice to play Esme Cullen?
Y or N

10) If you could be in the movies. which part would you like to play?
Bella, Alice, Rondsme

11) If you had to cast the movies with your friends, who would you
choose to play each part? same but I wou
be Bella

12) Which movie is better — *Twilight* or *New Moon*?

13) Which movie is better — *New Moon* or *Eclipse*?

14) Which movie is better — *Eclipse* or *Twilight*?

15) Which actor is cuter — TAYLOR LAUTNER or Robert Pattinson?

Name:

16) Which actress is prettier — *Nikki Reed* or ASHLEY GREENE?

17) Which actor is cuter — Jackson Rathbone or Kellan Lutz?

18) Which Twilight actor would you change places with for a day?
_____ Jacob Black _____

19) Which Twilight actor would you like to have visit your school?
_____

20) Which Twilight actor would you like to go to prom with?
_____ Edward _____

21) Which Twilight actor would make the best BFF? __Alice___

22) Which Twilight Saga movie premiere would you have wanted
to attend? _____ Eclipse _____

23) Which Twilight Saga actor would you like to have for a sibling?
_____

24) What is your fave song from the movie soundtracks? _____
_____

25) What is your fave scene from the movies? _____

26) What is the best quote from the movies? _____

27) If you could change one scene in the movies, which would
it be? _____

28) If you were the director of one of the Twilight movies, what
would you do differently? _____

29) If you could have one Twilight character's wardrobe, whose
would you choose? _____

30) If you could have one Twilight character's car, whose would
you choose? _____

FOR YOU AND YOUR BEST FRIEND ONLY

Nobody knows you like your best friend – or does she?

1) Would you be best friends with a vampire? Y or N

2) Would you be best friends with a werewolf? Y or N

3) If your BFF were a vamp, would she make you one, too? Y or N

4) If you were a vamp would you turn your BFF into one, too? Y or N

5) If you and your BFF could be in the TWILIGHT MOVIES, would you do it? Y or N

6) Which parts would you two want to play?_____

7) Which Twilight actor do you think would get along best with you and your BFF? _____

8) Which Twilight character do you think would get along best with you and your BFF? _____

9) Which Twilight actor would you like to have over for a SLUMBER PARTY? _____

10) Would you take you BFF with you if you got to meet Stephenie Meyer? Y or N

11) If you discovered you were a werewolf would you tell your BFF? Y or N

12) If you became a vampire would you tell your BFF? Y or N

13) Would you ever go CLIFF DIVING with your BFF? Y or N

14) Would you let your BFF give you a Twilight-themed makeover? Y or N

15) Which Twilight characters do you and your BFF look most like?

Answer the questions like you think your best friend would. Have her do the same for you. Then swap and find out just how well you know each other.

1) Would you be best friends with a vampire? Y or N

2) Would you be best friends with a **werewolf?** Y or N

3) If your BFF were a vamp, would she make you one, too? Y or N

4) If you were a vamp would you turn your BFF into one, too? Y or N

5) If you and your BFF could be in the TWILIGHT MOVIES, would you do it? Y or N

6) Which parts would you two want to play?_____

7) Which Twilight actor do you think would get along best with you and your BFF? _____

8) Which Twilight character do you think would get along best with you and your BFF? _____

9) Which Twilight actor would you like to have over for a **SLUMBER PARTY?** _____

10) Would you take you BFF with you if you got to meet Stephenie Meyer? Y or N

11) If you discovered you were a werewolf would you tell your BFF? Y or N

12) If you became a vampire would you tell your BFF? Y or N

13) Would you ever go **CLIFF DIVING** with your BFF? Y or N

14) Would you let your BFF give you a Twilight-themed makeover? Y or N

15) Which Twilight characters do you and your BFF look most like?

_____